10-20
P9-CLF-129

Florence and Her Fantastic Family Tree

To my grandchildren: Abby, Madalyn, Grace, Christian, and Radley.
—J.G.

To my lively nephew and niece, Luca and Beatrice.
—L.A.

Copyright © 2020 by Judy Gilliam
Illustration copyright © 2020 by Laura Addari
All rights reserved.

Published by Familius LLC, www.familius.com
1254 Commerce Way Sanger, CA 93657

Familius books are available at special discounts for bulk purchases, whether for sales promotions or for family or corporate use. For more information, contact Familius Sales at 559-876-2170 or email orders@familius.com.

Reproduction of this book in any manner, in whole or in part, without written permission of the publisher is prohibited.

Library of Congress Control Number
2020936665

Print ISBN 9781641702508
Ebook ISBN 9781641703703

Printed in China

Edited by Kaylee Mason and Brooke Jorden
Cover and book design by Carlos Guerrero

10 9 8 7 6 5 4 3 2 1

First Edition

OCT 30 2020

Florence and Her Fantastic Family Tree

By
Judy Gilliam

Illustrations by
Laura Addari

Childrens Department
Menasha's Public Library
440 1st Street
Menasha, WI 54952

At least Ms. Collin didn't assign us a diorama for the family project. She said, "Just create a family tree." Like that was easy.

The problem is that my family tree doesn't just have a trunk, roots, leaves, and branches. It has stickers, thorns, and extra limbs. My family tree is prickly, scaly, and partially overgrown.

may
FAMILY
TREE
A
A B C
a b c

My best friend Sonji's tree is pretty simple—one mom, one dad, and one brother. When she puts her family tree up on Ms. Collin's classroom wall, it will look like this:

But mine will take three or four poster boards and end up looking like a jungle of people. You see, I don't have a neat little family. I have extras.

There's me, Florence, and my brother, Fred. And we have four parents—well, make that six. You see my problem. How do I explain this?

Okay, first it was just my mom and dad—Betty and Bruce. They got married and had Fred and me. TA-DA!

When Fred and I were really small, they broke up, and then Betty married James and Bruce married Lucy.

Are you counting?
That makes four parents now.

My dad
BRUCE
SON
my brother
FRED
2ND wife of my father
Lucy
STEPMOTHER
my mom
Betty
DAUGHTER
ME :)
2ND husband of my mother
STEPFATHER
JAMES

Betty and James ended up adopting Caitlin, my half-sister, and Bruce and Lucy came up with three of their own, my half-brothers Wills, Brian, and Percy.

Then, sadly, Bruce and Lucy divorced, and Bruce married Kate while Lucy married Fabian.

DAD
MAMA
WILLIS
BYRON

If you're still counting, that's six parents: the original Betty and Bruce; Betty's second husband, James; Bruce's second wife, Lucy; followed by his third wife, Kate; and stepmother Lucy's new husband, Fabian.
A total of six—hard to keep up, right?

As you can see, my family tree is going to take up a lot of space on the classroom wall.

To add to the giant tree, Bruce and his wife, Kate, had a son, Sam, who is technically my half-brother.

That's a lot of kids.

There's me and Fred, then there is my half-sister, Caitlin, and the three half-brothers, Wills, Brian, and Percy.

Oh, and don't forget about new baby and half-brother, Sam. So, let's see what this family tree is going to look like now.

FRED
BRIAN
PERCY
CAITLIN
LITTLE SAM
WILLS

Sometimes, even I get confused about all my parents and siblings, so I worry that my teacher and all the students will be really confused too.

That's not my only worry—

Will my tree actually fit the space on the wall?

What do I do if it's too big?

Can I explain who is who?
Will anyone believe me?

Should I bring all of my
family to school?

No, let's stick to paper.

I may need help taking it to class
and taping it to the wall, but here goes.

My family with all the parts—
stems, branches, leaves, trunk,
berries, and nuts.

SAM

It might not be simple and might not be easy to describe, but these are my people, and they're going to take up most of Ms. Collin's wall.

But you know what the best part is?
That's me right in the middle of this
great, big, loud, colorful, fun, crazy
family that I call mine.

Next time, I'll include my grandparents—
must be twenty of them!